The Triangle Motel

L.B. Robbins

Copyright © 2020 by L.B. Robbins

All rights reserved. No part of this publication may be reproduced, distributed, or transmitted in any form or by any means, including photocopying, recording, or other electronic or mechanical methods, without the prior written permission of the publisher, except in the case brief quotations embodied in critical reviews and other noncommercial uses permitted by copyright law.

ISBN: 978-1-953048-72-1 (Paperback)

The views expressed in this book are solely those of the author and do not necessarily reflect the views of the publisher, and the publisher hereby disclaims any responsibility for them.

Writers' Branding
1800-608-6550
www.writersbranding.com
orders@writersbranding.com

Contents

Chapter 1 At Home in Sea Isle City	1
Chapter 2 Making My Plans	4
Chapter 3 The New Sports Car	9
Chapter 4 My New Neighbor Theresa	12
Chapter 5 The Boy Scouts	15
Chapter 6 At Lionsgate, The Retirement Home	18
Chapter 7 Angellica Plans Her Spring Garden	23
Chapter 8 Theresa's Heist	27
Chapter 9 All By Myself	30
Chapter 10 At Lionsgate Again	32
Chapter 11 Overseas in The Lagoon	36
Chapter 12 Theresa Remembers	38
Chapter 13 Our Story	41
Chapter 14 In Pago Square	44
Chapter 15 Terry's Never Ending Adjustments	49
Chapter 16 Back at Lionsgate Again	54
Chapter 17 Wes Travels	57
Chapter 18 At The Long End of The Faculty Lounge	60
Chapter 19 In the Final Stages of These Frantic Days	63
Chapter 20 Safe in the USA	66
Chapter 21 The Riddle	69
Chapter 22 In the Dark Halls	73
Chapter 23 The Chameleon	76
Chapter 24 Stephen's Thoughts of Li Chi	79
Chapter 25 The Gathering	82

Chapter 1
At Home in Sea Isle City

My name is Angelica Peterson and I live in the little shore town of Sea Isle City.

The sounds and smells of the sea combine with good sea food freshly delivered from the boats off shore. This is our town and this is what creates the backdrop for the recent storybook interest in our city.

My husband Rob and I moved here twenty years ago, after his retirement, to be near our only son Robert. He pastors the Lutheran church not far from here. Now I live here alone, but I see our son frequently.

We both grew to love this little village for its simplicity and blind faith in its proud people. The local monuments to its fishing industry all supply testimony to these facts.

Years of residents waiting the safe return of their hard working loved ones from the sea explain the history of Sea Isle City.

Why has no one heard of us? Why aren't we listed in the ten most visited cities of the United States? The answer is simple. That's just the way we like it, undiscovered.

Surprising things go on in the midst of our ho-hum life here. It is more than just a tourist trap, there is a genuine interest in history. A lot is happening. I don't ever seek any excitement, it seeks me.

L.B. Robbins

Enough kitchen philosophy, I'd better concentrate on the task at hand, buttering my toast and planning the jam to go on it.

About a year ago, as happens, I lost another one of my dear set of neighbors, the Blooms. The Blooms were a fixed part of our community, decent, hard working folks. I've just heard from them. They moved in with their younger children in Arizona. They love it there, they tell me, but it's just not home yet. Oh well, that will come in time.

The Bloom's house was a standard fifties style rancher. It was a "Sears" house, they said. These modules were very well made to be sure. The new young couple came complete with school aged child, eight or nine years old perhaps.

I watched as a dog and some furniture were loaded into the rancher from a large moving van and then breathed a sigh of relief that there was nothing unusual there.

It was all that could be expected of such a respectable middle class couple.

I waited a day or so and brought over one of my home-made coffee cakes, the lemon one, to welcome them to the neighborhood.

I let them know I would be there if needed, but otherwise "take your time, we move slowly here".

They were the Lawrences.

I learned that about them that day, that and not much more. They had many years of traveling with the navy department.

After thanking me for my thoughtfulness, we exchanged good-byes. With that, the efficient young man in the suit and tie turned on his heels and headed for his car. His wife seemed shy in a brunette sort of way, and apologetically explained that he was late for work.

The Triangle Motel

I had the feeling that she'd had much experience doing this.

I took my cue and left, with a senior citizen sigh of relief. How lucky could I get, no noisy outdoor parties with loud music, with only one child, and a well behaved dog that, if my luck held our, might stay out of my garden.

I think I'll plant blue bells this year. Yes, that might work out. It usually does.

Chapter 2
Making My Plans

This is the time of year that I start making my gardening plans. If I start early enough, there can be a small resemblance to the final picture in my mindset. Luckily I have enough perennials to create a sense of continuity. Yes, that was my final goal. I have a sense of what I call, "excuse me, if you want dynamic changes, you'd better look elsewhere." That is what attracts others to our community. That, and a better than average education system!

One day I had a visit from Robert, my son. He usually visits lunch time. A timid knock was heard at the door while we were sharing some of my homemade clam chowder. I'm very particular with it. No one shares my secret, though they've tried. Mrs. Lawrence, who told me to call her Theresa, wondered if we could help her with a small computer problem. Her class was this evening, she was late, and her husband was out of town.

Let me explain why she, my new neighbor, felt I might help out. We shared a driveway, and what a nice young man her husband turned out to be. He had helped me start my car. The battery was low, he said.

Stephen, her husband, smiled in a friendly way. He made the simple jump start and went on down the drive in his car and then off to work. What strange eyes he had! The left eyebrow seemed to rise noticeably in the air, then slowly turned right and joined the other. A cowlick, I think they call it. Nevertheless, it was friendly.

Of course I would return the favor. She sensed Robert might be able to bring her computer "up", as she called it, and asked if we could help. Robert has that intellectual look, he does wear glasses. He is more technical than I am, almost everyone is. I'm anxious to learn, however, since I've become the proud owner of a small laptop thanks to my son and daughter in law.

I tagged along dutifully and then snatched some of my apple pie and wrapped it in foil as an afterthought. I crossed the lawn and entered what once was the comfortable kitchen next door. Instead of the roomy early American kitchen of the Blooms, I found that this beautiful room was dedicated to some kind of a futuristic theme, Star Wars I think.

I had taken my twin grandchildren to the local showing of that strange movie.

I knew where I was. I had walked into a space ship which was traveling through space at the speed of light.

IBM had now taken the place of the cozy early American mood the Blooms had set. The only clue that remained that cooking should be done here was relegated to a low corner cabinet. A small stainless steel sink hid shyly next to it.

The focal point was a large double desk with computer equipment and a giant black leather swivel chair designed for a giant in the center.

I could picture her husband running his empire from there, swiveling in any direction at a moment's notice. Better yet, a large gorilla named Chu something.

L.B. Robbins

Robert brought "up" the system, as he called it. What a surprise! I saw eagles, a coronet of stars, a Washington monument, several naval pendants and a block that said "my homework". A snake made the plea, "Don't tread on me". It was a virtual panorama of patriotism.

Robert clicked on "my homework". It whirred and printed out some serious lines of text and we prepared to leave. Thanks were exchanged, we left and I wondered if her professor had any idea how little thought went into this project.

Later on Theresa was to confide in me that Dr. Levin, who was her professor, thought she must have been in "this business" for quite a while. He said so after class, having read the last weeks homework. "Two weeks at least" was her reply. "Then you didn't write this?" he said in amazement.

She offered to quit if he felt she was doing anything immoral or illegal, but he assured her he wanted to see one of these each week. "And oh, be sure to let him tell you what he's done and why." She promised faithfully she would let her husband do just that.

I noticed that the window, where the Blooms former sink was, remained intact. It was the same (and it was the only thing that was still the same).

There was one difference; the pale yellow blinds were closed tight. It faced my home.

I guess that told me what they thought about me.

When we arrived home Robert expressed his opinion. "I think we have visitors from Foggy Bottom, Mom." I didn't know what that meant. I didn't want to know.

The patio was covered in a tarp. I can only imagine what was under it. Poor Buddy must have been hushed away in a safe room somewhere.

I had been corrected about the collie, about his breed. He was not a collie, but a border collie. They were supposedly the most protective of all breeds. It turned out that Buddy had his work cut out for him!

Somewhere on the other side of the world, a development of very serious consequences was taking place. A concrete and metal building of moderate proportions was in the final stages of completion. Only the sound of the generator could be heard.

The modest enclosure was camouflaged with the native ferns and fauna available to the small compound. A handful of silent figures moved on the outskirts in their paramilitary gear. The sign said "Danger-Beware" in an unknown tongue.

What was going on inside was highly sensitive. It was important that no information was leaked to the outside through this thick jungle foliage. It was highly unlikely that it would be. There had been very little human penetration into these parts in many years.

It would be best to stay away, it was whispered. Some knew what had happened to those unfortunate enough to have shown too much interest in the project. Sadly, what had happened was not widely known by the locals. The word was, don't show too much interest in this project. It could be bad for your health.

Other than the small hanger on the shore owned by the US military, the site would have gone by unnoticed. It was usually not occupied, not by humans, mostly by marsupials.

Phase one was completed. All that was needed now were the military components.

This was already in the planning stage. Hardware was en route to complete the testing that would be needed for this top level project. The software was already there.

Chapter 3
The New Sports Car

I love it here in Sea Isle, nothing seems to happen very often, and that goes as well for my new neighbors next door. I thought so at the time, that it. One exception was the delivery of a dark green sports roadster. I don't know the name of it, but that is what we used to call it. It surely was exquisite, sleek and small, quite low to the ground.

The sleek green machine was lovingly steered into its new home in the two car garage by Stephen, its new owner. My nose was glued to the bay window in my kitchen, along with those of my two cats, Emma and Ursula.

The new purchase was carefully washed and waxed, though it didn't seem to need it.

It was Saturday, so father and son were both there to admire it.

I went out and looked over our short picket fence and congratulated the pair on the new purchase. Mr. Lawrence replied shyly that he'd waited a long time for it. It was an MG, he carefully explained.

All at once it seemed as if he regretted it, letting a stranger see behind the thick curtain he presented to the world, in the shape of a rather long wave of brownish hair across his left eye. I felt I should promise not to tell anyone else.

L.B. Robbins

They wasted no time jumping into the two-seater and headed down the winding paths our city provided. Poor Buddy had to stay behind, but he looked as if he was used to it.

Little Shawn looked and waved excitedly at the same time, "goodbye Mrs. Peterson". I didn't know the child that well, but a happier sight I'd never seen. They did some serious turns down the sloping path to the lush, green, never, never lands of Sea Isle.

Oh, and yes, another experience occurred within the same month.

My eyes were alerted once again to the same small bay window, thanks to Ursula, when an official dark blue car entered my driveway. Two men in dark suits and sunglasses exited their slim forms from the car and headed toward my front door. They first took a long look at the obscure rancher next door, expecting to find something sinister.

After checking their badges and photo IDs in their wallets, I let them inside, naturally. It seemed they were filling out forms for some sort of "security" application required by Washington. They were very impressive, and took pictures of my driveway as they walked toward my front porch.

They presented the drill. "No", I answered, "I can't not think of anything I've seen that could stand in the way of Mr. Lawrence's receiving this clearance," as thy called it.

As they were leaving, they asked me to suggest another neighbor for confirmation. I assured them that any one of us would be a witness to their suitability. We were all fond of good, quiet, families who didn't intrude on our sedate worlds.

More pictures were taken. They were really professional. Their equipment was very extensive for two civil servants who were merely checking on the suitability of a future member of the department of defense.

As if to complete the picture, young Shawn jumped off the yellow bus, greeted by his dog Buddy and was met safely at the door by his mother, Theresa.

I felt it was time to bring over the application for the Boy Scouts troop that was forming at the local Lutheran Church. Robert had dropped it off earlier.

The two men witnessed this fond display of family unity and silently must have agreed this cozy family was a shoe in for the position. I walked with them as far as the mailbox and left.

I was reassured that someone in our government cared so much about our security.

I thought they were the ideal family too, yes, a definite shoe in. After dropping the Boy Scout application in the mail box I hurried off.

Suddenly my suspicious mind saw something foul in this strange visit.

I didn't want to get into a discussion of why our government had to second guess its citizens. In short, it was an invasion of privacy.

Should someone be taking long range pictures through the garage window?

Chapter 4
My New Neighbor Theresa

Weeks passed, and I had occasion to meet with my new neighbor, Theresa. at our joint boundary line (asphalt, theirs, and clam shell, mine). Sometimes we would meet on one side, then on the other. The wide driveway we shared emphasized our differences.

Mrs. Lawrence waved and came over with a "Thanks" for the Boy Scout announcement. She, however, could not think of it at this time, it was impossible.

She'd recently answered an ad for our local Maritime Museum in the local Penny Saver, and they seemed interested. It would be part time, three days a week and unfortunately Thursday was one of those days. "The job is perfect." she explained. "I don't even think they own a computer. I feel completely safe."

Now, I had been the mother of an only child, and still am. I know how lonely it can be for these young folks. I asserted my information that our school bus service was very helpful and they might consider dropping Shawn off at the church. It was on the way, to my thinking.

At once I received the chilly look of an unhappy mother. I had crossed the line. It said, "I don't interfere with your life, leave mine alone."

I took my cue and drove off to the post office. This was definitely a lady who knew her own mind. I recognized a kindred soul when I saw one.

Spring was here and I had my mind on other things. My crocus showed real promise and the daffodils would not be far behind. I had a new gardener and Anthony showed real promise. He was fertilizing my small back yard and the grounds behind the garage, fixing the barbeque and removing the dead leaves of winter.

In a few words, I had enough on my hands and I could barely handle everything in my daily planner.

This year I might try an herb garden. I'd try fresh parsley at least. That was my favorite. I'll talk to Anthony right away.

I'll study the seed catalogues Robert and his wife had sent this way. That way Anthony will surely be impressed with my knowledge. I usually just purchase them full grown at the Acme.

While I'm making progress, I'll add a shelf to the side of the porch that faces the Lawrence's back yard and install a higher watt light bulb.

Plants in clay pots will need much care and watering while I check out the yard next door. I'll be ready the next time someone comes around taking pictures.

Someone might find themselves becoming a star in the new scrapbook I'm planning to put together. I'm planning to buy one of those phones that can be used for taking pictures. I'll have to consult with Robert, he uses one all the time.

Back to my garden! Yes, the clay pots, geraniums would look nice, with some basil planted around them. That should be attractive and easy to handle as well.

The shrewd eyes looked above the long nose to the yard next door, as the canvas lawn slippers stretched the tiny frame well beyond its five foot length. They would be prepared to face the battle that seemed to looming menacingly in the background below the surface.

Oh, and yes, rosemary, what was it they said about rosemary?

Chapter 5
The Boy Scouts

In about the space the space of a week or month, I don't know which, I was alerted to the presence of a visitor at the back door. It was Theresa, and a remarkable change had taken place. Highlights in the hair, a touch of soft blue eye shadow and a spring in her step, all of these made her seem like a new person. Oh yes, the glasses were gone. Emma and Ursula quietly moved upstairs, they knew the drill.

"I just wanted to thank you for the information on the boy scouts. Shawn is so happy. I think it's made a big difference. He doesn't take well to change."

"I wanted to drop off some Danish, prune and cheese, I didn't know which. He gets dropped off Thursdays by bus at the church. I need to know of a place to get patches sewn on, he can't wait to show them off. I really never did have a sewing machine. Can I use your phone number as an alternative emergency?"

She was in a rush, I could tell. She ran in and put the assorted Danish on my table.

I welcomed her change in mood. She must have been under a strain of some kind.

"Stephen is away again", she went on, headed for the door again.

"He's in a place called Pago Pago, I think. He called and said he wasn't sure where it was when I asked, "All these navy hangars look alike".

Stephen fixed their computer problem, which he was supposed to do. No, he didn't think he'd take a cab as I suggested and get to meet with some of the locals.

Theresa looked it up, she said, and it was in American Samoa. "We're so different", she stated. "I definitely would have spent time in that gorgeous place. It looks like a great getaway for tourists"

This was an unusual burst of information for Theresa, but I agreed to her assessment out loud, their differences. They were more alike than different, to my way of thinking. The perfect couple, not always found these days. Two very unique individuals, their ruts running around and into each other, they were a team more than a marriage.

I can't imagine my husband Rob being held up in a place like that without coming home without reels of home movies, and stories of the native foods and children.

I did see her starting the battery on his sports car once or twice so it would start when needed, but not driving it. No, there wasn't a secret sports car buff in her genes. Those two really were different. She loyally drove the grey Honda.

Still, I could sense a change taking place. Maybe the Honda would go the way of the glasses.

I had really become fond of young Shawn. He stopped in often to show off his new Boy Scout patches, sometimes with Buddy, sometimes not. I made sure my new cookie jar was filled with chocolate chip cookies. Robert enjoyed them as well, too well.

Shawn even shared one of his computer games with me. That was so cute. I could tell he wasn't used to sharing. Pieces of candy fell from above in various delightful colors all over the screen. He had no trouble installing it.

I was impressed. Shawn was so young. Someone had taken great pains to be sure he'd be way out in front of the pack. He did have that crazy eyebrow that his father had. That probably explained a lot.

Despite promises made to Shawn, I never touched the game when he wasn't there, though, once I've made a promise I usually stick to it.

Playing this candy game should prove interesting. I could impress the twins at the same time with my computer prowess when they visited.

I really thought our brief encounter together would just fade into the future. Years into the future, Shawn would be driving his own sports car. I would think of them as I thought of the Blooms.

Soon, Theresa and Stephen would move in with Shawn's new family in Arizona. The circle would not be broken, "bye and bye, yes, bye and bye". I thought of them, but not at all as I thought of the Blooms.

I was not wrong, they were a far more different family than any family I'd ever come into contact with, not the type to share a barbecue with on a summer evening. No, I've never met and would never meet another family like the Lawrences.

Chapter 6
At Lionsgate, The Retirement Home

The sedan headed up the long narrow dirt path as the driver mused "where in the world are we"? Theresa's eyes reached up to the GPS on the dashboard. She wouldn't have attempted the trip without it, she knew that for sure.

It was hard to believe, but Stephen had helped to design that curious gadget while on loan from the Navy Department, and he alone had planned the testing for it. Whenever she had to call him while he was out of town, she merely asked for the GPS section. She was transferred immediately to Stephen.

That was mostly while working at MIT in Massachusetts. All she had ever been aware of was the Triangle Motel. Sometime she'd like to take a trip there.

Sometimes, but not right now, she was so proud of him. Right now she was afraid for him. Where was this infernal spot she found herself in anyway? And why was he in Pago Pago? He was not in the CIA, he merely helped them out when needed, temporarily.

Suddenly a clearing emerged and she was unexpectedly viewing a large, turn of the century building, brick with large dirty columns that had once been white. Time had not been kind. The shutters were freshly painted blue, obviously the beginning of a work in process. "Lionsgate", the small sign at the foot of the drive, was the name of the building. It seemed unsure whether to announce it proudly or give up on it. From lack of direction it seemed to say "Enter here at your own risk."

Inside, at the same time, Stan Walthers was staring into a mirror in one of the second floor rooms off the large hall. What he saw was an elderly gentleman with wide grey eyes and hair to match. They both had been livelier in their day. "You're holding up better than most of us", he told himself critically as he struggled with his comb. "For those of use who've been put out to pasture, that is!" Yes, he was holding up.

The "Those of us" he was referring to was a small group of GS level somethings, all retired at the same time, all thought of as useless because they'd reached the age K Street considered over the hill. It could really hurt the ego, Stan thought, if you didn't know better. He could bring to the front of his memory unimaginable stunts he had performed, secrets he'd uncovered, no, thought Stan, we were the top of our class. Top Drawer!

It was decision time for this former agent; the biggest decision was what shirt to wear, with or without tie.

These days it could be critical, could force a decisive road down a path of victory or defeat.

"Who is this woman who had to see you so badly?" Nellie had whispered in his ear. She sneaked a giggle behind his back. True, she never missed a thing about her favorite "client".

"She's sure got you interested in your looks, sly devil!"

Nellie was right. It told him how crucial this visit seemed to be to him, this unknown person. He had nothing

L.B. Robbins

better to do than watch TV. He might as well do it. Yes, he'd go with the button down cable knit sweater. It matched his eyes, dead grey with wild strands of white sticking straight up and out from his eyebrows.

Her name was Theresa. There was something totally unknown about this name to him. Though he strained his mind to go back to his past, it didn't help. She'd travelled quite a distance to see him however, so he'd oblige and listen. It was the least he could do for the fairly large retirement check he was receiving from the government. Maybe it would help clear out the cobwebs that were closing in.

In any case, it would give him something to do before lunch.

Wives, he thought, where would the country be without them? The army used to say that if the government wanted you to have one, they'd issue one. Wives were usually the last to understand and the first to get upset.

He's never fallen into that trap, and now he could afford to say so. Sadly the only thing useful he had to read were the monthly account statements from his pension plan.

It was all he had to show his many years of devotion to the firm. But at least he had that, unlike his many friends who'd chosen on and off again marriages. Thanks to that one good choice he had made, he did have a solid bottom line to that myriad of papers that were called a portfolio. It was called profit to those who didn't know what an illusive gypsy she could be. It had been a strange ride!

Still, wouldn't it be nice to have children and grandchildren, to have some pictures on that lonely bureau against the wall. Stop it, Stan! That trail was pointless.

Who the heck was this guy, this Stephen something? These young bucks, so eager to outshine the others, so much competition, they were all alike.

You could get overlooked so easily, better give the hot shots a reason to notice you.

Show up the others, that was how he did it. Oh yes, early promotions. He's done it all. Until it backfired, that is. The law of averages said it would happen, and it did. Luckily he'd kept his job, for all the good that did.

The old juices were stirring. Maybe he could do this one alone. Yes, he'd already decided he's take it on, whatever it was. Better yet, go on the prowl with the others.

The game never ends, only the players change. Get the poker team together.

What was that motto, "we did what was needed" was the first rule. What was the second?

Though he tried to do so, he couldn't remember. He needed to get a cigarette and think about the story that this tragic young wife had just told him. If he was right, it was the same old thing. Her husband was spending more and more time away from home and money was missing from their accounts.

He had one cigarette left in his shoe, time to steam up the shower. An alarm went off on his expensive sports watch. "Darn, time for a blue pill", or was it yellow. Better take both. Stan sighed and slowly slipped forward into the boring life he had not prepared for.

Maybe it was just what he needed, this strange case of another husband who seemed to be breaking the rules with a wife who was beginning to figure it out.

Later that evening: "Time to hit the stairs and face Nellie again", he thought cynically. Theresa had just left. He offered only one piece of information. "Give me your cellphone!" He promptly removed the Sims card and replaced it. "Be careful!"

Stan watched the slim figure exit the room, looking shaken and defenseless. In a flash the old fears returned. Yes, the familiar story, it was no wonder this shapeless, haunting cloud that hung over them never ended well. The structure of the story was stubbornly the same, someone was missing, someone very important to the weapon in question.

He'd looked up Theresa's husband in the top secret, classified files he had no real right to be looking in. Yes, his fears were well founded.

Now, he remembered it, the second rule, "don't get caught." Why did it take so much longer to remember things? It happened to other more normal people, but he'd always thought he'd be an exception.

He looked up at the stately winding staircase. It was the pride of the owners, not the staff and not handicapped compatible. Maybe he'd wait for the small elevator. He'd do the exercise thing tomorrow and think of this strange case after breakfast.

The wise, grey head shook slowly, stared ahead, with a "Here we go again."

Chapter 7
Angellica Plans Her Spring Garden

I was back in my hometown of Sea Isle studying the aphids on my azaleas, which were just about to bloom. That could ruin my big plan. It was a Thursday and Robert was here visiting. We were consulting together about the azaleas, and just about to go inside for some lunch. I had prepared some chicken salad and vinaigrette greens.

Theresa appeared on our incongruous driveway, and she was obviously distressed. She had been crying.

"Would you both please come over and let me show you something?" We did so immediately; this was so totally out of character for her. The look of grief told us so.

We entered through the back porch off the kitchen and went right to that strange computer center that was set up. Theresa turned it on and once again went right to "my homework". A message came up on the screen that said in bold script. "Do not print this out".

"If I do not come home on Friday, take my car to Van's sports cars in town. Ask for Ed Rivers and him alone. Tell him to get into the car, face the auto center, turn right, go five eighths of a mile, stop the car, get out and open the trunk. Let him look inside. I'll be in touch."

L.B. Robbins

She was obviously upset; she didn't know how to drive that "infernal thing" as she called it. In her state, she shouldn't be driving anything.

Just to calm her nerves, Stephen offered to drive her and she was so relieved. They drove off with resolve in the MG toward town. I took the opportunity to look inside the pantry the Blooms had been so proud of, their latest addition. It was to hold their large freezer and the jars of homemade jams and jellies they shared with the neighbors.

What a surprise, the refrigerator was there, but instead of glass jars full of delicious treats there were tapes, hardware and very neatly wrapped extension cords. What had Robert called them, hard drives. Each one was tagged and dated and reflected the unusual mind of its owner.

Everything about the pantry was neat and orderly, it could almost have been called a "clean room" that I'd seen in some movie. No signs of food anywhere. There was also a Star Wars poster above the tiny stainless steel sink in the corner, a new addition.

The poster had a guy with a blaster and a scantily clad princess.

Not the usual homemaker's kitchen. Definitely not the usual pantry!

When Robert returned home, the first thing he said was "Mom, you meet more strange people in a week than I meet in a lifetime."

"I have to tell you, I meet a lot of people. These Trekkies sure landed in the right spot".

"Well, tell me?"

"Tell you what exactly?" Robert said.

"What was in the trunk?"

"All Theresa saw was a Western hat and a laptop next to it".

"You know, Mom, I think it might have been lucky that I was there with Theresa."

"Frankly, I'm not sure what would have happened if she'd been alone. The next time, if there is a next time, we slow down. We figure out the best plan, then we figure out the safest, and whatever the safest is, that's the plan we take."

"In any case, this is not normal. I expected tools in the trunk, not a laptop. Was I ever wrong!"

"Do me a favor, talk to Theresa, Mom. You have a way, that nice way of finding out what's really going on. She won't even realize she's being grilled by an expert."

"All right, but I don't think the poor child really knows what she's doing, or why."

I handed him the lunch we had planned to share in my kitchen. I had packed it for him, with enough for the twins, and, of course chips and soda. He headed home right away.

The next day, to no one's surprise a white van appeared in the drive with some kind of security letters such as "AXC appeared. They spent quite a while making Theresa's home safe.

I could never have anticipated this. Of course I never could have. My husband Rob and I had led the sedentary life. He had been a stock broker and we would never have had the need of a security agency. Robert's theft, the one he'd had in the past was quite a shock to all of us. But that could never happen again. Or could it?

The following week, a replacement was made.

L.B. Robbins

The new van, which was totally without any advertising on the side, took two days to complete the chore which their competition had done in one day.

It was white without letters of any kind.

It was not that I was nosy, but I sensed that with all going on around here, it would be better if I moved my small table and rocker to the front porch. That way I could do my cross word puzzles out doors and check to see the young child safely home at the same time.

I had taken over the trimming of my forsythia which placed me in hiding when the school bus arrived, and this put a pair of sharp clippers in my hands at the same time.

The family must be in need of tighter security for some reason. It was not the thing young families spend their money on, trying out new security agencies. This new agency had taken two days to complete the security. They were obviously better.

I knew without giving it too much thought that Theresa's husband had not been satisfied with the choice she had made. Better let the experts take charge, he seemed to be saying. Those eyes, those blue azure eyes, I felt they could be cruel and cold, friendly and warm on a moments notice.

Why did I feel that way? There was something about the confidence he possessed.

"Angellica, quit making judgment calls! You don't even know this man."

Something only years of experience, and the far away look in those blue eyes told me all about it. That strange kitchen of his should have told me that!

Stephen Lawrence had learned to face the world as he knew it, and he knew it very well!

Chapter 8
Theresa's Heist

On the surface, as I expected, things were chugging along safely guided by some unseen hand, a hand which, I was hoping, never left His position but was steadily on duty.

Our little street was unchanged in any case. The driveways between my neighbors and I were still mismatched. Theirs was paved, mine was ground up seashell. One of the local fishermen provided for many of us. Once the smell drifted away, and that took a while, it was quite attractive. It was quite a lucrative business for Mr. James.

Spring was still working its magic. The forsythia was quite glorious, the azaleas were ready to bud," the play was at hand!"

I was sure I needed a security service for quite a while, but Robert assured me I was safe for the time. There were no high level secrets taking place at my home.

"You know, Mom, you don't always have to rescue your neighbors. Some people just enjoy them or stay away".

One day, I don't know which, a blue Ford truck appeared in the driveway next door. I also don't know how long it had been there. Emma and Ursula were on alert, so I walked over to my bay window to see what was going on. Theresa and an elderly gentleman appeared from her side of the house and he was carrying a computer. Theresa waved, she saw my car and knew I'd be watching. I knew that whatever it was, it was "safe", she was letting me know that.

I was happy to see a new spring in her step. Was the hemline a little shorter? Something was different. Oh, dear, that husband of hers had better get home a little sooner than he was expected. If not, we might have a real situation on our hands. She seemed to be shredding his computer. What would be next, the marriage?

Why was Theresa doing this, removing his computer? After having two security services making sure her house was secure, what was this all about? Did she not trust one of them or both? I had to admit once again, our thinking was not the same.

I had never even had one security service. Theresa had hired two, and she still wasn't satisfied.

Later on, she let me know what it was about.

She had quit her class, didn't have time for it and didn't like it in any case.

She'd gotten a call from the pentagon and they announced they were coming over to remove Stephen's computer. That was fine. They owned it, they could have it.

They could not have her homework, however. That was her business, and it was all on the same computer. The Maritime Museum exchanged it for one of theirs.

What could happen? At least her homework was safe.

The museum was fine with the exchange, according to Theresa. Cruz, who was from the museum, had been there for several years and he had no problem storing her computer and letting them baby sit an old one of the museum's.

As Mrs. Peterson listened to Theresa's story, her very wise thought was "Of course she had simplified the story to them. She does things like that."

Did anyone else have a kitchen decked out like a rocket ship?

Chapter 9
All By Myself

Not everyone had to know about her silent fears concerning the strange things happening in the last few weeks, Theresa told herself. Not even Mrs. Peterson.

I came home tired, but feeling a lot better about my new neighbors next door, as I prepared for bed.

I recognized now that I was behaving with a little too much confidence. I thought I had everything in control. I was so wrong!

I had just made arrangements with Stan at Lionsgate. We will meet over the weekend, and he assured me I was imagining the difficulties Stephen was having. These things happen all the time, he assured me. I have this strange feeling he knew all about my situation, or at least the ones just like it.

When Stephen was safely home, he could sort it all out and remove my homework safely. Stan was the one who suggested I put his computer in safe storage. I was thinking that after a few paychecks, a new one could be purchased. By the fall I'll own my own computer, plus a few other things.

My mind was beginning to drift off to the many things I'd only dreamt of. End this fantasy right now girl!

By the fall, that was the question! Who knew what would happen. Things were taking on a life far different from the one I'd always prepared for.

Would we all sail away safely in our dream sloop toward the rosy horizon? For the first time, I just wasn't sure.

I was sure of one thing however. When Robert was kind enough to drive me to the foreign car repair shop, I knew right away that there was a message from my husband in the two items in the trunk. One of them was a white hat. He had always said, when I questioned the wisdom of one of his many travels, "Relax, Honey, I'm with the good guys in the white hats." That was enough for me.

I knew that laptop was bogus. That was all I knew. Something was up for sure. I couldn't wait to see Stan. The little I knew of him, I knew I could trust him. Along the way, many of us have had to. The long lines in his face and the scar alongside them suggested this.

Chapter 10
At Lionsgate Again

Back in the common room at Lionsgate, a plan was being devised.

It was the Wednesday poker night at the old soldier's home. Stan was sitting alone, preparing how he would present his case to his three friends. The cards were sitting in the middle of the table ready to be dealt.

Stan was the only one who didn't drive. He couldn't in any case. His doctor wouldn't allow it because of his heart. Two of the group had been with him for a long time, twenty years of so. Wes, the youngest was still with the firm, but had grown attached the last few years to the "grumpy old guys", as he called them.

They used to meet at the old farmhouse Wes rented. The couple who had owned the farm for years thought this was the nicest group of men, these friends who enjoyed game night at their farm.

Harmless, they bragged to the neighbors and they were so quiet. One of them was working on a computer program for the blind. For the most part, they explained, they enjoyed games which had to be acted out. None that they had ever hears of. Something about dungeons or some such thing, they recalled. Nothing violent, they mostly talked all night.

The boys arrived on time, as usual.

The Triangle Motel

Stan was looking around the room, as was his custom. He had silently swept the room for anything intrusive, checking all security points that could be breached. His eyes never missed anything, and now wasn't any different.

An attempt on the stately old dining room had been made to give the appearance of an international center. Prints were hung on the walls of various foreign capitals, interspaced with sailing ships for emphasis. A large picture window had been added to give the impression that they were not locked in, however no door had been added, should one of the clients, as they were called, attempt to leave.

The cards were already dealt. The boys walked in quietly and took their assigned seats.

Stan wasted no time. "Have any on you ever met a Stephen Lawrence?" No one had.

After giving it some time to sink in, he further added the news that had interested him.

"Well, he's disappeared. His wife was here last week and I told her I'd ask around. It's not unusual for him to be away, but it was her son's birthday. He's never missed that before."

"Oh, hell", Wes said. He knew what it all meant, he would have to track down some information for these guys. He was the only one still working at the firm, and he was the only one with ties to the files. It was risky, not nice being caught! He had been doing things way above his pay grade.

Stan still had a computer in him room. His internet had been disabled after some pressure from above.

The only thing he was allowed to play was three handed solitaire and Tetris.

The word was out that he was planning to build his own connection to the internet, but it was all talk, as it turned out. Someone had noticed small deliveries from the local hardware store. It was Nellie, that infernal nuisance, as he lovingly saw her.

As Stan looked under the table he saw the leather tote bag placed there by one of the three. It could have been any one of them, they all lived by the same rules. He knew what it contained by the shape. It was a new laptop. Either Wes or Jessie had brought it.

It contained powerful new software.

Stan had devised a plan where he could bribe one of the handymen to drill a small opening in the baseboard of the tiny visiting room next to the office.

He could run the cable all by himself on a Saturday if he had the right tools.

If, and it was a big if, these arrangements were followed, there was a carefully measured cable inside the bag with the laptop. He had to be very careful.

He always looked to the past, and he missed that big rush that had ensured his meteoric rise to the top. The innocent look he managed to cosmetically apply worked all the time.

Yes. He could still do it again. This soft life left nothing at all he was interested in.

On reflection, he could now recall the meeting that Theresa had been talking about. It was the Institute of Navigation annual meeting, where he had was being honored for forty years of service with the firm. It was held in Chevy Chase, Maryland.

Because it was so close to the capital, it always attracted celebrities. In this case, it had been the admiral, young Sikorsky, who was the grandson of the inventor of the helicopter.

Yes, he could recall Theresa, she shared the head table with him. The young couple were very quiet. Her husband had volunteered as program chairman.

She had helped chose the speaker for the young man.

She had confided that her husband had been busy and didn't have time to line up a speaker, and she had done so.

All he could remember was that something had scared her, and he promised that nothing could ever happen to her while he was around.

"How will I find you?" she had asked. He wrote his cell number on the program provided.

He had had no idea that she would save it.

Strange girl! "No different than anyone else in this room" Stan thought. There were a bunch of strange ladies around, as the dinner had been made public.

"Sikorsky psychics" Stan had called them.

Who had brought in that strange character that had nothing to do with navigation?

Yes, it must have been that person called Theresa.

She was not at all the typical military wife.

Chapter 11
Overseas in The Lagoon

In the dead of night somewhere near Pago Pago in American Samoa, a Cessna Skylane 182T was flying low over the waterway approaching the small naval hangar. The sun had not broken through yet, but the two young pilots in the cockpit knew the area by heart.

It was the only thing that broke the monotony of their monthly tip to nearby Pago Plaza for marketing their homemade Samoan shirts.

There was never much activity at the small hangar, but this was different.

Better call it in. There were no signs of life in the small tower, only two flashing lights seemed to be limping dimly on their own.

They couldn't smell it, but they could see burning embers behind the hangar. Something very large had been towed, although the tracks had been filled in. They could not have known. The raid by the locals, or someone else, had just happened three hours earlier.

Stan Walthers knew all about it hours before they knew it. They just didn't possess his talents with his new hardware setup. Picking up the noise was easy. What was not easy would be telling Theresa about it.

He had to sit in the comfortable armchair in his room and think about the next step he had to make, and then make it very carefully.

One of the few perks of retirement after a long career between himself and the top military brass over the years was a close handshake relationship.

He hadn't used it much over the past, but he didn't feel the need for using those long switchboards in the halls at the pentagon. He'd played golf enough with them at the most exclusive clubs in the DC area.

He was trying to remember which of them were navy and which of them sported the most scrambled eggs on their shoulders behind their high desks.

One came to mind immediately. He wasn't exactly on his speed dial, but very few in this privileged set had this particular number. Yes, they owed him one!

When the phone was answered, Stan said "I've got someone you've got to meet."

Chapter 12
Theresa Remembers

Theresa was studiously reviewing that strange meeting she had just had with Stan Walthers at his even stranger retirement home, Lionsgate. Although Stan couldn't remember her, she, Theresa could never forget that night.

It had been three years ago. She had spent quite a while getting a memorable speaker for the event. She really owed Stephen one. The last quarterly meeting had been, Stephen felt, quite a failure. She thought the group needed a little diversion. She had been busy as well, so she lined up a hypnotist that she had met at her gym.

Apparently these people were serious about sticking to the subject. She had enjoyed his presentation, but Stephen had very definitely not. He might have been a little jealous.

This time, since she'd failed last month, she'd do a little more research, and she did. Everyone was excited about meeting the great celebrity Sikorsky. He was most interesting. It took a while to set it up, and she discovered he was a gifted psychic as well. Their turnout was quite phenomenal for the small group. A very popular member was retiring as well, which accounted for the increase in their usual attendance.

That is where she met Stan Walthers. The dinner was to honor him. He was seated next to both of them at the head table, which is where they usually sat, so Stephen could introduce the speaker.

There were many visits to the head table, accompanied with drinks for Mr. Walthers, which probably accounted for his exuberance, when a most unpleasant thing occurred to her.

An elderly lady approached her with a somber message. I supposed it was one of the psychics. She was attracted to a ring I was wearing, one given to me by my grandmother. She asked if she could examine it. I let her, and she replied ominously "Don't ever remove it dear, it's the only thing keeping you from a very serious disaster in your life. This ring has crossed many oceans, its only purpose is in keeping you alive." The dark creature silently headed for the back of the room.

That is when she and Stan spoke for the first time. He'd heard what she had said, and promised his protection should any evil befall. He signed her program with his cell number, when she begged him to. When she returned home, she placed it carefully away in her little desk, where she kept her valuables.

This time, when she retrieved it, she also brought out the antique moonstone ring which she had set aside, from her Grandmother.

Stephen had given her a pearl ring for Christmas. She felt she should wear that one. After her recent scare, she recalled the dire warning, and slipped it back on her hand.

That should do it! Thanks Gran. Gran had also told her the same thing. Nothing bad can happen to you while you wear this. Don't remove it!

She was a believer now.

Oddly enough, the hypnotist turned out to be quite a bonus. Stephen was able to hypnotize himself into sleeping

L.B. Robbins

with his eyes open, which helped at the pentagon (where he spent many hours waiting for the higher and very popular officers). It worked in church as well, she'd seen it.

Most of the church members were impressed with his complete attention to the sermon. I alone kept him from the deep snore that would have appeared without my intervention.

I had two functions in life. One was to hold up my end of the conversation around the table when we had guests. The other was to keep Stephen awake during the sermon.

It was not always easy! Nothing about her whole life was easy.

Especially now, when it seemed her whole world had turned upside down. Stephen's office had called, not his immediate supervisor but the base commander. This was serious.

I could never forget the exact words which he had rushed through out loud, as if he were reading from some scrip he was never comfortable with.

He said, after some hesitation, "Your husband has contacted a virus out of country, and it will be necessary for him to stay in sick bay for several days. We will be in touch."

I looked up at the wall above my son's desk. A new poster had been delivered by special overnight air. I hastily put it on the wall with thumb tacks. A small green guy with luminous eyes and a bald head was saying "May the Force be with YOU!" May it be with all of us, was my thought.

How can I keep my son from hearing about his Dad's illness, and his being away at the same time? His father was Shawn's whole world, his hero and mine too.

Chapter 13
Our Story

Our story is not very different from the many couples in our set. Stephen and I met in college, where our fraternities and sororities got together on occasional weekends. My purpose was selfish, I needed a math tutor.

My high school, an all-girl's academy, had never prepared me for anything beyond socially acceptable mathematics. I can still add and subtract very well. The lucky girls in this academy had no use for math. They would marry well and produce sons. End of story.

When I got to college, it might as well have been Greek, this thing called "college math."

Now I have never been a quitter. I joined a group of my friends for a visit to the Pi Kapp fraternity house, which contained all the engineers and the rest is history. It was a magical evening, it was Halloween, and the spirit world was out in full force. To say it was love at first sight was oversimplification, but it was just that.

Years later, I asked Stephen why he had never offered to do my homework for the easy forty dollars I flashed around very noticeably. He had this to say, "I always knew I'd be doing your math for the rest of your life." Quite gallant! I had to marry him, and yes he was always very gallant. He also, I thought, looked like Robert Redford, although no one else did.

During Desert Storm, Stephen had made some quite important contacts while stationed there, and he had already landed a job with a hardware company, Sperry something. We travelled ten years, after which we both wanted to settle down in a good school district.

We chose Sea Isle City. It seemed perfect. It had the sea all around it. Stephen's hobby had always been sailing. We never had the money for a class sailing sloop, his dream vessel, but we had plenty of time to study them. The school system was ideal, and until our dream arrived, we could enjoy the pretty neighborhood, and its many class sloops.

The perfect little house had everything we wanted. There was one problem, and that was our new neighbor, Mrs. Peterson. Was I imagining it or did she want to know a little more than was necessary.

Because of the nature of Stephan's job, I was naturally suspicious. Most people ignored us because of our tendency to be aloof.

Maybe I was just too used to moving often. Maybe I just didn't see any sense in getting to know the neighbors. It was painful parting from so many faces that I hated to leave.

Chevy Chase had changed my thinking, I really hadn't wanted to leave. Couldn't we try, just try to be like normal families?

This quiet town seemed to be our best bet for doing just that.

I was going to do my best to put our life on a new trajectory.

We were getting romantic overtures from MIT, I recognized them. Invitations from the faculty for expensive dinners, plus plane tickets and reservations in four star hotels were offered to reel us in.

It hadn't worked. Stephen was too conscientious to accept their generous offer while he worked for the government.

Stephen insisted we pay our own way, and that might have been what kept us continually working for navy. Something had done this in any case.

I secretly thought he loved his job. They let him take over the controls and fly during testing. He didn't have a license. You don't need one in the military.

It couldn't get any better that that!

Chapter 14
In Pago Square

In the middle of the busy square in Pago, a strange middle aged figure was coming to life. It was Jerry, the master sergeant who had accompanied Lawrence on this journey to American Samoa. The trip had been a disaster, and he had been the grunt assigned to assist him with these strange instruments, some kind of computer equipment.

All he knew, and he didn't know much, was that they had both been kidnapped by some crazy locals for a reason that he couldn't imagine. All it took was a lapse of 10 hours in the time for the normal shift of troops to provide security.

Some kind of high level activity had occurred, and Steve Lawrence was the celebrity who was to lend his magic to the event. Unfortunately they were not there to participate. They and the weaponry had already been kidnapped. It had all happened so quickly.

To tell the truth, he had a great respect for the man, which he'd developed in the last forty-eight hours. All he knew about him was the wedding ring he wore. He was even quiet about that, although he stared at it in a strange, metaphysical way.

They weren't allowed to communicate in any case, but they were able to use eye contact, and the bright master sergeant knew something was going on in Lawrence's mind.

He was cooking up something, that was all he knew, and he was encouraging Jerry to get away and spread his story to the right people, under that crazy left eyebrow of his.

This was a guy you could never be sure of. Something about him said you could count on him in an emergency though, and this was surely an emergency.

As soon as he could walk, he'd find the nearest provost marshal and do just that. He must have been drugged. He had his freedom and that was enough to be grateful for.

Meanwhile, Stephen knew he was the only captive left in the compound. They didn't need another mouth to feed while they were carrying out this dirty deed, these desperate people. That meant two less guards, and that would lead to his successful escape. He assumed the attitude of passive but compliant tech head.

Unnoticed, he was able to destroy the code. The time of his escape was close, and, if the indications were correct, he'd better just watch and wait for his appointed rendezvous. The carrier Harry S Truman was already here with its f18s. The radar screen told him that. Someone back home must have intersected the strange code he'd managed to dispatch to the states. That itself was a miracle, the first of many.

Others most have noticed too. Part of the crew of natives had cleared out.

Once all the equipment was out of the compound, it could be destroyed. He knew one thing. If he wanted to see his wife and son again, he'd have to put on the best performance of his life. Not caring, that was what counted with these people.

He knew he could get rid of one of his guards this way, he'd had enough time to put a plan together, and it was this.

Stephen was determined to make his ten o'clock departure. That was the only way to make the appointed time of the extraction written into this code, this crazy code that had just been transmitted. Just how much had did they know, the folks at home?

He had spent his time figuring out the coordinates of the raid, and the easiest way to get to them. Thanks to a lucky change he'd made to the code while in design stage, he had included a patch to determine his present whereabouts. His background had been after all in surveying. He gave the impression of being distracted at the time. He was actually determining the coordinates of his present location.

The old location of the equipment on the beach was already stored, thanks to that patch.

He could be stubbornly determined when he had to be. He knew now he had to draw on his many talents.

All he had to do was get to that lonely shore at the right spot and time and start a bonfire.

He had a lot to make up for to Terry. I promise, Honey, things will be different when I get out of here! No more listening with one ear instead of being a part of her difficulties. The god of second chances had to help him.

The sergeant that had been taken away had managed to hide a dagger under his nasty bunk before his removal. He didn't know how, but it was the only way to get rid of his Samoan guard. He had managed to smuggle a dead rodent into his room in his small cell.

This poor fellow had to be created into an object of interest to distract the overweight ninja who would be making rounds tonight while he, Stephen, hid behind his door. His guard's right pocket had the shape of a German Luger, and Stephen had to have it. He had to get home, that was the highest instinct he possessed at the time. If he had to, he'd do the unthinkable thing.

Whatever it took, that's what he'd do. He'd remove the Luger from his ninja's right pocket. There wasn't too much he didn't know about guns. He'd designed one for himself at ten years old. He had plenty of time to think about it, and many years of nine fingered typing for all his trouble.

Meanwhile he checked his pockets for the stale crusts of bread he'd stashed.

More time was what he needed. He knew the seals' plan would be flawless. Don't screw up now Lawrence!

Success had come too easily and too fast. The military had recognized his talent early in the game. He was sent to the military's crack computer schools in Maryland with a flawless record that surprised everyone. It was something Stephen had become used to and he wasn't aware of it as a child. Not everyone possessed it, his strange DNA code.

It had positively bewildered his earliest teachers. What would become of this unusual child? Who could have guessed this particular scenario?

Now was the time to draw on this curious talent of is, now more than ever. Yes, time to spend with the family. Stephen prayed for that precious commodity. He sharpened his new knife. His blue eyes were sharper now than that knife could ever be.

Once he was out of the compound, he had to move fast to be sure his disappearance wasn't noticed. He knew one thing. If he wanted to see his wife and son again, he'd have to put on the best performance of his life. Not caring, that was what counted!

L.B. Robbins

He sharpened his new knife. His blue eyes were sharper now than that knife could ever be. It would not be wise to underestimate him right now. It would be his loss, this unfortunate native.

Hours later, he was able to drag his exhausted body to the nearest shoreline, he hadn't been missed yet, at least!

Luckily there were the dying embers of a fisherman's campfire, and it looked like seals crawling out of the water, they'd seen it too. He yelled "It's me"! It was the last thing he remembered.

Chapter 15
Terry's Never Ending Adjustments

Back in the small Sears home in Sea Isle City, the fevered pitch had melted down to a small simper in the homeowner's mind. Theresa had heard officially that Stephen was on his way home. He would be checked out in at a military hospital first.

Now that Terry had entered this totally new and frightening season of her life, she had a new appreciation for her neighbor, Mrs. Peterson. Shawn had never failed in his ability to seek out sincerity in those around him and then attach himself to them when he found it.

He found it in Mrs. Peterson, who knew she always managed to be on her front porch or near it when his bus returned from school. Shawn knew that if her car was parked outside the garage, she was inside. She encouraged him to stop in her kitchen if he wanted company.

He did this often on the days when his Mom worked. She wouldn't have felt secure at the Maritime Museum if it wasn't that that dear lady would be there for him.

She felt bad now that she'd had portrayed a different personality when she first met the Petersons.

"I'm afraid I lied a little about the day the white van appeared. I didn't know Mrs. Peterson enough to confide the seriousness of the situation I was in. Now I know that I can do so, and I will, without any hesitation", she told herself with conviction.

She recalled that the first van was one contacted from the phone book. The second was a van that Stan Walthers had secretly sent to scope out the area, as he called it.

He had sent a colleague of his named Wes.

They were both alarmed by her message. After Wes searched out Stephen's hard drive, as he called it, he was even more worried.

"He's got some pretty serious stuff on this. I'd better call Stan".

He did so and passed the phone over to Terry. Stan seemed to have come to a decision. Although his whole career had been a series of one deception after another, he broke with tradition and told Terry the whole truth. He had decided she could handle it.

Then he decided they should get the computer to a more secure area until Stephen was home to take care of it himself. His words directly were, "We'd heard he'd gone off the grid" meaning Stephen of course. "Don't worry, he'll be back. Trust me!"

Not what Terry was hoping to hear at all, that Stephen was still missing, and not in sick bay.

She trusted Stan for some reason more than the officials at this new base, she didn't know them at all. His voice comforted her.

He passed on the news that no one from DC had checked on Stephen's security clearance. He'd had it too long.

"Don't let anyone into your home. Check with me first."

Wes was leaving. He promised to be back soon with better news. He'd surprise Shawn with some games.

Terry did as was directed. The computer in question went to the Maritime Museum. Trust for these people was complete. They had made her feel like a part of their family, for some strange reason known only to them.

Stephen's computer was safe. Stan told her how to turn the cameras off while they made the exchange. Meanwhile a complete reexamination of feelings for the people next door was taking place.

Robert was truly a gift from heaven, he was so caring about Shawn. He didn't have to go out of his way at all to get Shawn accepted in the boy scouts, but he cared so much. He cared for a young child who was alone all afternoon. Robert must have been lonely as well. It wasn't just that he was a minister, there were many of those, but he took to it like Father Christmas.

"I thought his concern for his mother was overblown. Surely her greatest fear ever could have been that her cheese fondue had failed to rise properly! I was wrong about that, very wrong. It was no mistake that providence had put her here."

Terry knew that those sharp eyes of hers didn't miss a thing. She noticed her new ring right away, and even asked about it's being very old and very rare.

Also, she remarked about a tan car that seemed to appear when the school bus did. Terry should have paid more attention to her. Now she knew, too late, she was right.

"In the future I'll be careful to take her observation seriously." Shawn was not here now.

Mrs. Peterson had followed the bus on Thursday, which was boy scouts day.

L.B. Robbins

When the tan car slowly followed the bus around the corner, she followed it at an even slower pace.

She crept carefully behind in the shadows until she saw where it stopped.

The car stopped right at the church, just as she, Mrs. Peterson had feared it would. She maintained her slow pace until she saw the police station in view.

The police checked it out, they knew Mrs. Peterson well. "Following a bus full of kids?

That doesn't look good. In New Jersey your license plate has to be clean, no mud on it." Step inside while we check you out." They took him inside the station.

He had never been seen around town again.

Shawn was now staying with Pastor Peterson in the next town and being driven to school.

"Stephen, I miss you too!" Terry looked down at her husband's blue robe which she was wearing, while sitting in his favorite chair. It didn't help at all. She had somehow known this day would come.

Looking down at that strange ring didn't help at all. Yes it had helped comfort her, it reminded her of her Gran. Gran knew somehow that this day would come.

Stephen had known too.

All of a sudden, she realized why he had insisted she take those strange courses. "You know you could never live alone on the part time salaries you make, Terry."

Her fear was that there was another woman back in the shadows, although she couldn't picture it. No, she couldn't see that outcome at all.

Only Buddy was here now. Faithful Buddy.

The Triangle Motel

The dark sense of fear that had been hiding in the pit of her stomach was making its way slowly up her spine. In all the years she and Stephen had been together, nothing like this had ever happened. She was the only one who knew where Shawn was., she was better off.

Mrs. Peterson had suggested it, no, insisted on it. So they both knew. What was in this tiny lady's past that had given her a clue that she herself had missed completely? All of a sudden, she wanted to know Mrs. Peterson better.

Suddenly, she knew she could sleep at last. Had the herbal tea worked its magic or was it the realization that she had a new friend next door.S "Come here, Bud." The small border collie snuggled right up. He seemed to sense his new role in this strange situation.

Chapter 16
Back at Lionsgate Again

It was a Saturday morning at Stan's retirement village, but not at all in any ordinary sense of the word. Stan was in the very special small visitor's waiting room away from the heavier trafficked main reception area. It was designed to provide privacy for those families who were experiencing very intense problems of a personal nature. It had an inexpensive lock that could be broken easily should the need arise. This gave those unfortunate families the false feeling that they were in control of their distress. It was locked right now.

Stan pushed his chair away from the wall and stood up and stretched his aching back. So far his work had gone undetected. That at least helped the little success and slow growth of his project. He had uncovered a plot so devious and monstrous. It was able to shatter that thick protective wall he had built around that unique being, Stan Walthers.

Stan had managed his way up from intelligence officer in the Air Force. He had a choice of Washington DC or Colorado. He picked DC. He career had flown skyward ever since. Soon he was able to pick and chose targets at random, and he chose this one.

What he had been able to pick up from the noise that was hovering around the case wasn't good. No one without the lifetime of experience he alone possessed could have extracted what he had. It was the Triangle Motel again. He'd been afraid of that.

Stan's extensive investigation of Stephen Lawrence told him he wasn't dealing with the ordinary GS14. He'd been in at the ground level with the Triangle Motel, and all the way through to the patriot's testing.

Of course passing off Wes's ID codes as his own helped uncover a lot. He had shown Wes how to maneuver in the shadows far above his security level. It more than helped, it alone made it possible.

He was trying as hard as possible to keep the young man safe. The top level wasn't fond of loose lips who, they felt, had betrayed the code. The fact that they had failed to protect their own secrets was completely overlooked.

Terry had touched some sympathetic nerve that hadn't come to the surface in years. She brought back memories that were better left buried. They'd spent quite a bit of time on the phone. Not her phone, but they always spoke on the marine museum phone where she worked, and a different one each time.

He had been emphatic about that one.

She was used to following agency rules, and that is what Stan put his trust in, a good career wife.

She was now allowing him to call her Terry, very few people did. Of course, Stan's cell-phone was "safe". He'd seen to that fact years ago.

No one could have it done it better than Stan. Why had he been so interested in this strange case?

As he stretched his long frame, he was pleased with his own expertise. So far, no one had noticed the tiny hole in the baseboard. Now he carefully withdrew the almost transparent cable.

He shouldn't need it for a while, hopefully not at all.

"You haven't lost it, young man." The old pride in a job well done returned. "Now you've earned that cigarette." He reached into his shoe and headed outside where he could contact Wes.

It was important that he contact him in time. Wes was on his way to the Triangle Motel.

He had big news for Wes. He'd picked it up himself from the white noise he's zoned in on while "traveling" in the area in a local CIA substation.

Yes, it was the Triangle Motel, the motel that was code for a continuous missile operation being conducted at MIT.

Chapter 17
Wes Travels

The not-so-white Trailblazer was traveling northward along Interstate 95 at a pretty good clip. No reason to alert highway patrol, so Wes kept to the speed limit. It would be good to get there on time. A lot was at stake, but a steady hand and a cautious one were what were needed at this critical time. It was also critical not to lose the dried mud he'd applied so carefully right before he left. It gave the impression of duck hunting.

They were planning to meet at an obscure diner, which never attracted attention, the food was not spectacular. It was a perfect decoy. The story went something like this.

The ambush had taken place a week ago. No one at this time was sure who had done it, but a small rebel force had invaded the naval airport. Everyone had a good idea of who it probably was, but as yet there was no proof.

It had started about 18 months ago, as far as anyone knew. Tight confidential code had been removed from MIT. It was naval missile code of the highest security.

The theft had gone unnoticed right at the time, so no one knew the date. It was completely well organized, a daring and successful theft of great planning, by someone inside. Inside what, was the real question? Was it MIT or a treasonous inside plot within the government, no one knew.

The rift could not be publicized. The highest levels of the government were alerted, and they alone, because of the secure nature of the theft. The seventh fleet and Norad were alerted. Because of the sensitivity of the parties involved, or thought to be involved, it was best to proceed cautiously.

Here is what happened. A paramilitary commando raid occurred on one of the offshore islands of American Samoa. Stephen and one of the contractors were targets of the raid.

It could be that they weren't sure which of the two Americans were targets of the raid. Since they didn't know, they took both.

This is what they were sure of. Testing of the missile was taking place in the area, per the satellite evidence supplied. According to interested parties, precision was off for the accuracy of the trajectory. The paramilitaries involved had demanded a patch be sent to adjust for the trajectory malfunction.

At this point they would return the two Americans.

This is what the assumption was. Someone who knew the code had adjusted it and convinced the rebels that they were too close to the equator, which was the reason for the new code.

The designers knew that distance from the equator had nothing to do with the design of the missile. They assumed at the Triangle Motel that this was a message from Lawrence letting them know he, Stephen, was controlling project testing, temporarily at least.

The sign for the exit was ahead. Wes turned off on to the exit, looking for his destination where the exchange would take place. This information was so necessary for the success of the mission referred to as the Triangle Motel. A sketchy reference, all in code, accompanied the papers, to be given only to one person of interest and to him alone.

Wes was proud of the plan. Theresa had given him the idea, and he had put the idea into Stan's head. From there it had gone on to the intelligence community. Its simplicity was its brilliance. All it needed was speed and a lot of luck.

"Talk to my brain, Stan." It was at this point that he was aware that he was lucky enough to be an acquaintance of one of the most spectacular minds of the twentieth century. Possibly the next century as well! How do you become that way? He wished he knew the answer. Was it a gene play or was the plan designed up above.

The Trailblazer turned into the small, obscure diner. Wes was relieved that his old partner was already there.

They were alone in the parking lot and that was good karma. Once inside they silently chose a corner booth in the back.

This alone would seem strange to the casual observer, but it seemed there were none. No words were exchanged. They were both dressed as tired fishermen, who'd given up for the day. After carefully studying the empty room, they ordered breakfast.

Wes slid the envelope across the table without making eye contact. Some other time they could catch up on details of their families and small talk. After what was calculated to be a sensible amount of time, they turned quietly and left.

The envelope contained no instructions. It was a copy of new patch of optional code written in Ascii.

Chapter 18
At The Long End of The Faculty Lounge

The long darkly lit hallway led to the last of the faculty rooms in the dining area. This particular room was chosen for its suitability to the plan. It was functionally small and dimly lit at the same time. It was the only one with a keypad. A nondescript figure in a trench coat entered after the appropriate code was entered.

The scholarly figure behind the stark desk looked up as the expected courier entered. He placed the official looking envelope on the desk with a satisfied look of "well done" on his deliberately neutral face, that typical face that seemed to be the favorite of the CIA.

He unsealed the manila envelope. It contained mostly what he expected. It was a copy of what had already been transmitted. There was one exception to the official code.

Every tenth Ascii instruction contained a Swedish word. It had been determined that probably no one that close to the equator was fluent in Swedish. It was Stephen's native tongue.

When the Swedish was strung together, the time of the rescue, coordinates and dates for a seal extraction were revealed. It bought much needed time.

Hopefully the raid would have occurred before the optional Ascii code could be examined!

Back channels were indicating there were conflicting pressures coming down from the leadership above among the Samoan natives. This seemed to be occurring down the whole east coast as well.

"This confusion could only add to our advantage", he thought to himself.

Plans were being made for a seal commando raid at last!

The rescue was being carefully planned, there could be no room for error. The highest level of the government was involved in working with the seals.

Suddenly he looked down as the truth sadly hit him. They'd been seriously infiltrated and it was dangerously successful. There would be trips back to the mainland and trips to jail as well for the infiltrators. He hated this kind of decision. He'd had to make too many of them.

He leaned back in his swivel chair which brought his focus to a picture of the pentagon.

Nothing about the wall, that olive drab wall, stirred the same the same feelings as this picture.

This sight of the central feature, the flag, always pleased him.

He knew what was happening right now. That squirrel's nest was being obliterated to discourage these rogue pirates from any new efforts to replicate the raid on the hangar.

Either secure the area better or destroy it. Best to make it just that, a stopover outpost to other more important sites.

And yet, that busy mind never stopped thinking. He loosened his tie, and unbuttoned his top bottom. What would be next for that tight little island? It was not an accident that he was three cousins removed from George Patton. He smiled again, a rare motion for him.

His eye fell once again on that flag, that flag he had done so much for, unthinkable things that they didn't discuss in the polite society down the hall.

His eyes of flint remembered, yes he would do them again. In fact "they" were doing it right now!

Yes, endless possibilities for the little island, after they taught these damned natives a lesson, that is. That thought brought another rare smile to his strange face.

Those dirty parasites won't mess with us again!

Chapter 19
In the Final Stages of These Frantic Days

Theresa sat alone in her living room. She had been assured that there were unmarked cars outside her home. This news had been passed along by her new friend Stan, once she told him that her family lived on the west coast. She didn't see much of them for this reason. There were other reasons too, but it hurt too much to think of them.

This call was made to Stan from the Maritime Museum in a seldom used room upstairs. When she felt she could disappear unnoticed, she slipped up the concrete stairs.

An incident occurred which had put the call in motion. Stan knew that she didn't call to make idle conversation. The pentagon had called informing her that they were planning to pick up Stephen's computer. It would be soon.

"Don't trust any calls that come in through your home phone,"

"Do you have someone you trust who can stay with you for a while? It would be best if you go to a motel if you can't think of anyone."

Yes, she told him, after he asked.

Shawn was away in a safe place.

Theresa didn't tell him where, and he didn't ask.

"If they call again, these people who say they're from Washington, tell them to come right over.

Try to sound as if you need the company".

Theresa knew she did need company. More than she'd ever needed anyone, she needed someone now.

She and Stephen were close. They hadn't felt the need for anyone but Shawn and each other. This was the natural result of traveling with only one another for comfort for such a long time.

It was fun at first. She had loved the anticipation of the next assignment. A new location and each new location came with a nicer apartment. This was how it was at first. It had gotten old.

Better get back in the present. If there was someone in an unmarked car, they were good.

They'd know where she'd be.

She'd let them know.

Bringing groceries to an elderly neighbor in need seemed innocent enough. The new location would be obvious when she banged loudly on the door, and she did just that!

It seemed Mrs. Peterson had anticipated her visit. She rapidly answered the back door which was brightly lit with the new bold globe Anthony had installed..

The area had been recently designed with no large shrubs nearby. Once again, he had done a good job. She alone of all her neighbors knew why Shawn wasn't home.

Mrs. Peterson had her small room ready for Theresa. In fact, it was always ready. She was one step ahead in her plans for rescuing her new neighbors. What kind of people would try to kidnap an innocent child? She shivered in horror at the thought.

She alone, once again, had spotted the unmarked cars in the dark street.

That couldn't be a good sign. It caused a twitch on the left side of her face.

People who knew her better never stayed around long when they witnessed that sign!

Chapter 20
Safe in the USA

The long ordeal was over. The little group in the Sears house were very somber, but joyfully so. Robert had led them in an earnestly grateful prayer of deliverance. Was it over? No, not for a long time!

All three had their eye on the large picture window on the front of the house. The drapes were wide open for the first time in a long time. Shawn would be arriving by yellow bus at any moment. He insisted on being there to protect his mother. He had two patches now and one of them was in lifesaving.

Robert had conducted a trip last week to the Maritime Museum. He felt Shawn needed to be kept busy. It had been just what the doctor ordered for the small child. A small group appeared in uniforms and all of Troop fifty would receive a new badge for the trip. The small scout troop were privileged to see exhibits the public had not seen, all because of the new guide, Shawn's mom. Trooper Shawn was so proud.

Stephen was safely and secretly secured in a naval hospital. Theresa didn't know which one, although she had spoken to him on the phone. That was the first time she believed it at all. She talked to him again, then again. Now she was sure he'd reach Walter Reed in Maryland.

The raid on her home several nights before went off smoothly, but it could have gone another way. The parties in both dark cars had caught the intruder just as he was preparing to break open the back door of the garage. It was silently and professionally done. None of the neighbors noticed at the time.

Theresa had both of these friends next door to thank for her safety. They seemed to take it in stride. "Doesn't this happen every day?" Robert walked in first, to make sure it was clear to enter when the men left. Once they checked out the house, they both insisted she sleep next door, while they remained awake.

This was her news. Stephen's physical was turning out better than expected, he was ready to return home, and really eager to. The navy would like a little more weight gain.

That was all they would say. "We'll be in touch."

The best part was, he was being granted early retirement and was taking the job which the community college had offered. They'd been holding out the offer since April.

The board was ready for him to start immediately.

Hopefully, that would happen. If Theresa knew her husband well enough, it was what he needed.

Stephen had finally accepted their offer. Theresa's comment over the phone had been, "Stephen, there has to be a better way to make a living than we've done over the past ten years!"

He had to agree. He would also be a volunteer at the Maritime Museum and build a computer system that would put them in competition for first place.

"Please Stephen, we like it just the way it is!" she'd responded over the phone.

L.B. Robbins

"Oh, and don't you have something else to say?" Mrs. Peterson slyly asked. She'd noticed the Zaleks furniture delivery van outside. They specialized in newborn furniture, and it looked like a crib.

Theresa blushed. She told them her news. The baby would be born in summer.

She told them the story about Stan Walthers and how he had helped get her through these tough days. It was an unbelievable story. She wasn't sure her neighbors entirely believed her and she could understand why they wouldn't. Who lives like this? What about this agency who wanted to know if she wanted her homework back? How did they know where her homework was?

She couldn't decide whether to wait for summer to send the new family photo to Stan. He had confided he'd like some family photos for the top of his empty bureau. How do you thank someone for rescuing your husband?

Yes, it was a perfect family. Soon to be a family of four, a rich man's family, they used to say. These days it was the last thing she hoped for. They didn't need riches of any kind.

Please keep Stephen safe. That was all she asked.

Oh, and wasn't it time to remove those beautiful walnut cabinets from the garage and swap them for that large desk in her kitchen.

Stephen no longer had use for it. He'd be busy at the Maritime Museum, spending his free time changing diapers. She'd use Shawn's small desk for her homework and Stephen would be in the garage to do his.

Chapter 21
The Riddle

It was late June and the perfect weather for a barbecue. Stephen was preparing chicken in the new smoker. He'd already designed a new cover to speed up the smoking process.

There was a strange look of contentment as he looked over his new purchase. He was seeing it for the first time. A home you could spend a lifetime in. May these people he loved never know the meaning of the smoke he had just witnessed in horror!

Shawn was shucking corn on the cob for his new friends, the Peterson's. They would all be there. None of the other neighbors knew there was a cause for celebration. Stephen's whole military life had been like this. The key phrase was this "nobody knew".

I was setting the newly purchased redwood table with plastic plates. I'd chosen the larger sizes, both plates and table. Flowers were already there, the usual suspects, sent over from next door. No hot house flowers, please!

My two boys had surprised me with a new lounge chair and they insisted I stay in it while they did all the work. I'd agreed to that readily.

While resting comfortably, I was in a position to look up through the maze of the chestnut leaves clear up to the highest exposure to the blue sky. One exposure lead to another,

I was way above the tree line. Now I was able to figure out the riddle. It had really puzzled me.

It all started with the poster on the wall "May the Force Be with You!"

This force had many parts to it. In my case it did at least.

It started right here in my neighborhood with the Petersons, who protected Shawn and I from the moment I met them. It spread to that strange poker night of the roundtable at Lionsgate.

Then it traveled as far as Boston to the Triangle Motel, where that strange force defending our nation in its own unseen way was located. It was unseen by most of us, but not by Stephen, Wes, or Stan.

I have to get to know more about it, but I doubt they'll let me.

The only clue I know is through the scout troop at the Lutheran Church. What I really want for us is what the Peterson's had, this faith.

Could anyone have it?

We'll find out together. He'll be on his own, as far as staying awake during the service at least.

It's time to take out that little book of Gran's from storage and take it with me to services. There's some kind of key to it all in there.

It was also starting to make sense, reading that strange programming code. What was really scary was that I was fascinated by it.

Now I realized what I should have known all along. I had miraculously married one of the few people who knew how to make sense of that truly foreign computer language.

He was able to use humor to draw comic characters to explain the mind of the complicated being called a computer. "Oh no, Mr. Bill"! At that Mr. Bill would fall off the edge of the logical world.

Only Stephen could relate to that tiny being with humor that most other people were afraid of.

His new students would be very lucky, they just didn't know it. It took me a while to figure it out as well.

Finally, we won't wait seven months to see Stan again. It would be the first thing the three of us would do, take that trip together through the woods to that elegant but run down retirement home that was Lionsgate..

There and only there could I find that brilliant mind this strange century had produced. That mind was Stan, and that was what Stephen would surely have become if he stayed where he was. He won't do that. I'll make sure. It was that simple.

The difference would have been that I would be rocking beside him on that large front porch, in that crazy future miles away!

He would be whispering in my ear, "Mental midgets and gnomies" completely out of range of the unsuspecting middle earth people surrounding us. Then he would turn that magic smile on to them to assure them that he was not very different at all. They usually all bought it.

The few that didn't, usually did in the end.

No, Stephen and I chose a different path, a path of helping young minds find their way to uncovering the crazy puzzle.

Stephen had unlocked a unique key to solving it that was safe, fun and creative. That, and, oh yes I loved him and always had!

Shawn chose a different path. He wanted to write science fiction. He was very determined and I was sure he'd do it. I'd spotted those halfway finished novels in his room.

As for me, I have a date with my new neighbors next door. Please always be there for us.

Here they come now with a casserole of some kind. Buddy is meeting them.

Ah, yes, a safe future! That's not too much to ask, is it?

I looked down and stroked that strange moonstone ring on my finger. Thanks, Gran.

Chapter 22
In the Dark Halls

The soft soled shoes walked carefully down the dimly lit hall toward the even darker stair wall to the unnumbered door in the recesses and away from the traffic. The only thing that was marked of any interest was a keypad of some length. A new confirmation code appeared below it. The same number in a different construction, to be determined weekly, this would open the unmarked door. Someone thought it would solve their IT theft problems. Maybe it would.

The shadowy figure secured the leather pouch under his left shoulder as he entered the codes with no hesitation. He opened the door and entered the room confidently, knowing he had not been observed. He'd taken every precaution.

He switched on the light and dropped the pouch on the large, empty desk. He let himself fall gracefully into the swivel chair. It had been a long journey and he sighed with relief as he looked up into a picture of the pentagon that so many others before him had looked up at in awe.

He'd found it hard to turn down the offer. The assignment had been divided into three personalities. It would take that many to fill the shoes of his predecessor. It wasn't for the prestige. No one would know the magnitude of the office he had filled. No one had his qualifications.

L.B. Robbins

His immediate assignment was to go through endless files to see if he could identify any of the countless transfer students who might have been showing too much enthusiasm for their assignments, especially to this project, which was classified. The next assignment would be to track down those who had been directing the hiring of these unique, high IQ individuals from outside of the USA.

It was tricky dealing with foreign nationals. That wasn't likely to happen again soon. Who'd made that decision? Another step backward, and even more difficult was to find out exactly who it was and why.

Who had traced the triangle steps from Boston, to DC and finally to Waltham, Mass. where the hardware was designed? Visa checks would begin in the morning on planes, trains and rentals. Could he put a number to a name?

The investigation had begun. Now it was time to kick it into high gear.

Next he opened his attaché pouch and read the new specs. It would be difficult but very interesting.

At that he looked through his strange blue eyes with the mismatched eyebrows down to the kids below in the quod.

Mental midgets and gnomies, every one of them, he was thinking.

"How can I tell Terry about this new assignment", he thought. She'd leave him for sure. Maybe a new sports car would impress her, but he didn't think so. No, not at all! A class racing sloop might do it. No, he remembered the look on her face when he'd said "Honey, no one just walks away from a job like mine!"

No one did, did they? Who else but he could put a name to a face. He'd been in it from design to inception to testing.

He had a fantastic memory for faces and for that chance encounter with someone who had no business being there, but had shown up anyway.

Better not mention testing to Terry.

He had no choice. He looked up again at the Pentagon on the wall and the flag flying proudly above it.

That said it all.

Chapter 23
The Chameleon

The room in the hotel was plain, clean and secure. As a backup to the plan, it fulfilled its function extremely well. Not too many visiting students or their parents were apt to select it because of its distance from the university and lack of appeal. It shared some of its unique characteristics with its present occupant.

This occupant was special agent Wes Seymore, recently of the Poker Players Friday Night fame at Lionsgate. There was a lot more credit given to this agent than he openly claimed from those select few who knew of his part in the rescue of his new boss. In fact almost no one knew of it. That was the down side of the career he had chosen. It was a lonely profession.

Wes was a specialist in counter terrorism and special ops and he was very successful at his chosen specialty. His conformist looks that were neither memorable nor eye catching were the reason for his many favorable outcomes that were never expected to succeed. Most people forgot he was involved in any way, and that was just the way the military liked it. It didn't fill the void that most people seemed to want to satisfy. In short, he was constantly in search of another occupation that would feed his ego.

The fact was, he was completely forgettable. He possessed a face that could be old, young, clever to dimwitted depending on the operation. He was an expert actor, and could carry out any role with ease.

Wes was the product of a racially mixed marriage. His mother was, and still is Asian. His father had been a high ranking army officer who was not always with them at all times.

Special agent Wes Seymore was known by many other names, mostly oriental. Although he was born in Canton, Ohio, he chose an obscure village outside of Hong Kong as his place of birth.

He'd been placed by Special Ops in Hong Kong many times due to his high ranking graduation from the military language school resulting in his fluency of the dialect of Hong Kong. His record was excellent.

The name that he had chosen for this assignment was Li Chi Chow. It had worked well in the past.

Makeup and his chameleon facial features would allow him to blend in as a slightly impoverished clerk in the admissions office at MIT who did nighttime cleaning and maintenance as well.

He would start tomorrow after his meeting this morning with Stephen Lawrence, his new boss, after disconnecting the camera at the kitchen entrance. Perhaps it would be tonight. Timing was important. He'd already spent time adjusting to his new situation.

He would be given lists of grades and activities of carefully selected students transferred within specific dates into the engineering department. Their grades were well above the ordinary. Wes was impressed. Maybe their high scores represented a reward for a favor of a different nature. Better check out those faculty members in question who gave out those generous grades so readily..

No one who observed him would guess the nature of his assignment by his general appearance. It was best not to overdo it.

Up until this year, he wasn't sure of what he did want to do. Since his trip to Sea Isle City he was beginning to feel the stirring of a need for a family, a home and a profession he could be proud of. Yes, a wife. He would know her when he met her. She would be sweet smelling and he would have someone at home to cry if he was missing. Someone he could bring home to his Mom. In the past the one's he'd met wouldn't have passed her litmus test.

He had wanted to be an architect, now he had the offer of help getting into a school if his mission was a success. That was a greater incentive than they knew.

Still, he had to work fast. He was scheduled to be the new head of the engineering department next week. It would be difficult. He knew nothing of engineering. Stephen wanted as few new people as possible in on this assignment.

The old department head was off on an unofficial holiday in the hills of Colorado, out of communication with his comrades, of course. No one was sure of the trail exactly or whether or not his wife was with him.

Only Stephen Lawrence knew. He was claiming no knowledge of the fact.

Chapter 24
Stephen's Thoughts of Li Chi

Stephen sat alone on his small bed in his motel room. It was nearly dark. He'd finished his bagged take out, smoked a cigarette, drank cold coffee and drew the blinds.

He'd already called Terry. She and the boys were fine, or so she claimed. She might have had a feeling that he wasn't being truthful when he claimed he was serving as a talent scout for the community college. She knew a little bit about the college and they had no trouble attracting kids.

He'd have to make it up somehow. A quick resolution to this problem would help. He was really pleased with Wes. He didn't know him that well. They made a five dollar bet that Stephen wouldn't know him in the cafeteria at one o'clock tomorrow. Stephen sure hoped Wes would win, but he doubted it.

He felt he was close to finding out who the turncoats were. Stan had narrowed his search down to those who had made contact or travelled to two geographic regions which were experiencing similar noises to Pago Pago. They were both in the Phillippeans. He threw both sites into the mix. They were now being discretely evaluated by covert ops in the DOD.

L.B. Robbins

Back at Lionsgate, Stan was rewarded with his own communications room, previously set up for family visits of those who were having problems. It now had a much more secure lock and it was designated a storage area. It had even higher level codes and programs installed. It was a minor dream come true.

Stan's room on the second floor was not a good option because he couldn't justify such a lock. It was circulated that he was experiencing headaches and required long period of rest in his room.

In fact, he had never felt better. Only someone with his background could understand it. He was now allowed more time outside and this allowed him to talk with Stephen on his cell. Only low level aids and lobbyists in DC were within his scope of listening devices.

This was his biggest complaint, but nothing could be done about it. Still, you never knew, you could hit pay dirt this way.

Stan, with Stephen's help, had narrowed down the old list quite a bit with more selective data. They were closer than ever to finding their culprit. These lists were about to be transferred to Wes on a new laptop. Wes knew the rules, only use it after hours at the university when no one was around, when he was in evening dress, that it, cleaning apparel.

Still, he'd experienced a bit of luck. The general, his golfing buddy, in response to his horror at the captivity of Stephen, was spending time of his own studying the playtime habits of the highest level ranks of the military.

The general had already uncovered strange details that made no sense.

Stan had provided the software material to guide him in his search.

It was basically an unauthorized search of country clubs, yacht clubs and private clubs that were visited very little by the lower ranks of society. Only those who kept guest lists were included, as well as some high priced eating establishments that only DC had. That was what turned up surprise information to the general's eyes alone. He'd better be very careful with this data.

Best to keep this one under wraps for a while until it could be verified.

All were within the confines of the triangle, all were repeated with the same members who'd also appeared in searches accompanied by the same guests. All had similar interests.

Strange bedfellows indeed!

After Stan made a mental study of his conversation with the general, he went outside for his evening stroll.

When his call was answered, he repeated to Stephen all of the details the general had passed to him about his new search. At this point Stephen made the same observation that he, himself had been thinking.

"Why don't we include the Chineese embassy at the United Nations. It probably won't amount to much, but it couldn't hurt. I'll see if I can reach Li."

They both said, at the same time and with the same intensity "diplomatic immunity"

He hoped Li hadn't gone to bed for the night.

Chapter 25
The Gathering

Terry was busy applying the final touches to her culinary masterpiece. It was Chicken Marsalla, the only thing she had ever taken a course in. The occasional business dinners she was obligated to preside over more often called for something special. She hesitated to deviate from its success.

Many of her new friends at the Maritime Museum were opposed to eating beef, and she couldn't remember which ones did and which did not, so this was her best neutral choice.

The beautiful kitchen now had the newly reinstalled walnut cabinets, with the addition of an official gourmet gas stove which now claimed the supremacy it deserved. It featured an oak table of her family's which she had hidden in the garage.

It was such a beautiful day, probably the last of the fall days that it would be possible to spend outside on her patio. She was preparing the fresh basil for the homemade potato salad to accompany the chicken, which Mrs. Peterson had brought over the day before.

She had invited her and, of course, Stan Walthers and his friend Wes. Some of the folks from the Maritime Museum had promised to come.

She couldn't help but think of the last time she'd undertaken a patio party. Terry had been so busy with the new baby, and had gone back to work as well. She finally fit into a smaller size sun dress, newly purchased. Yes, she felt pretty good!

She hadn't managed to let on to Stephen that he hadn't fooled her one bit. It assured the success of her party. He was out picking up supplies. She hoped he'd be back soon.

"Here comes Mrs. Peterson with Shawn, cookies and Bud", Theresa was thinking out loud.

Wes and Walt were pulling up in a dark blue BMW. She didn't know that it had been leased, and Terry hardly recognized Wes.

Wes, she later found out, had a custom tailored Italian sports jacket, matching hairstyle, and of course designer jeans. She knew little of his ability to slide in and out of character. Tonight this boy from Canon, Ohio was a film star.

"Here come the group from the maritime museum, everyone but Stephen", she thought. This was the reason she didn't like entertaining. He always disappeared before hand. She should have made appetizers.

These thoughts were no sooner out of her head than the MG pulled up into the driveway with someone she didn't recognize. He had on a rather worn out golfing attire, and a plaid rimmed Alpine hat with a feather in it. Walt rushed to the car, reached out his hand and shook it. "Hey, Jimmy, you son of a gun," and they were off together to the side of the garage.

That had to be the general. Mrs. Peterson had already figured it out and the three of them were consulting together already.

L.B. Robbins

This is what happened. Their hunch had paid off. The final party to be uncovered with the general's help, turned out to be a colonel's wife. The couple were living far above their means and were not really "Hamptons" material. Wes discovered this, as he was investigating the summer home of the colonel and his wife. They had surfaced on his list of Washington elite, who weren't born to the occasion.

It led quickly to the trail of a UN attaché who was often in their company. They all simply rose to the top of assorted students and a department head who did not readily blend in with the rest of the faculty.

Wes, or Li, found the group of marine biologists he had gravitated to much more interesting. Especially one with an Italian accent, named Liz, who he claimed had the "sweetest smell". She claimed it was a scent called Mussolini something. That couldn't be right, but it sounded beautiful.

She was surprised that he recognized her hometown, outside of Naples. It was a town that was not usually visited by tourists. She would have been even more surprised if she knew what he was really doing there.

Wes quickly changed the subject.

She wore a Bon Jovi sweatshirt and shorts and had legs that only a diver could possess.

That could really prove interesting!

He though he'd hang around a few days. He'd considered telling her that he was head of the engineering department at MIT, but Stephen would have frowned on that idea.

Speaking of Stephen, it was about time, but not here, to collect on that five dollar bet he'd made.

Wes had been working behind the counter at the line of cafeteria workers. He could keep his head down and still survey everyone who entered. He'd discovered that trick a long time ago.

Everyone was busy.

The general was saying to Mrs. Peterson, "It all began with a piece of gossip I picked up at the officer's club."

She answered "It usually does."

If the general thought he knew what she was thinking, he was wrong. It was something about the Blooms, and the fact that they'd never had such an international collection of such prestigious guests at one sitting.

Cruz Ruiz was admiring the cable bundling under the lilac bush next to the garage and he was really impressed.

Stan Waltham was discussing this week's episode of star trek with Shawn. He'd put a lot of study into it for the occasion. Shawn tried to trip him up, but he had no idea who he was dealing with!

Terry looked over at Stephen who was smiling for the first time in a long time. He really did look like Robert Redford tonight. She didn't look too bad, herself. And the baby was having his first overnight with the Petersons.

Little Cruz had better get used to traveling if he was going to stay with this family.

Why did she feel this was going to be an unusual night!

www.ingramcontent.com/pod-product-compliance
Lightning Source LLC
LaVergne TN
LVHW040158080526
838202LV00042B/3214